D1217594

NOTHING

JON AGEE

Otis's Antiques & Things

LLY'S
OYS

SAM'S
GIFTS

HYPERION BOOKS

FOR CHILDREN

FOR LUCIA

All rights reserved   Published by Hyperion Books for Children, an imprint of Disney Book Group
Library of Congress Catalog-in-Publication Data on file   Reinforced binding   Printed in Hong Kong
First edition, 2007

IT WAS ALMOST FIVE O'CLOCK. Otis had just sold his last antique. He was about to close up shop when another customer walked in.

It was Suzie Gump, the richest lady in town.

"Goody, goody!" she said. "Now, what's for sale?"

Otis looked around. "Uh, nothing."

"Nothing?" said Suzie. "How much do you want for it?"

Otis was baffled.

"I have a lot of things," said Suzie, "but I've never had nothing. I'll pay you three hundred dollars!"

This is ridiculous, thought Otis.

Then he remembered the words of his father . . .

Otis grabbed nothing and carried it out to Suzie's car.

"Thank you," said Suzie, and she handed him a check.

Otis was stunned.

So were the shopkeepers across the street.

"How'd you do it?" said Wally.

"Unbelievable," said Sam. "Three hundred bucks fer nuthin'? That only happens in the movies!"

In fact, it happened again the very next day.

Suzie Gump was back.

"Nothing is wonderful!" she said. "I must have more!"

"But, miss," said Otis, "I can't sell you nothing!"

"Very well," said Suzie. "I'll find it somewhere else."

Wally was waiting for her.
"Yer in luck, miss. I have the finest in nothing."
Sam called from next door. "I have nothing imported.
Nothing from Italy! Nothing from China!"

Well, it didn't take long for everyone to hear about Suzie Gump's obsession. Buying nothing as if it was something? She was nuts!

But then, maybe there really was *something* to nothing.

If so, there was only one way for people to find out.

Soon the whole town was in a frenzy.
Nothing sold like nothing before!

People quickly ran out of space.
In order to make room for nothing,
they had to get rid of something.

Otis was thrilled.

He found more things than his shop could hold.

But business was bad. People didn't want things.

They wanted nothing.

And, in less than a week, everybody had plenty of it.

Over at the Gump mansion, Suzie called her maid.

"Rosie, could you fetch me a towel?"

"There is no towel, madam," said Rosie.

"What about a bathrobe?"

"There is no bathrobe, madam. There's nothing."

"Nothing won't do," said Suzie. "I need something right now! Bring the car around to the front."

"There is no car, madam."

So, still wet, Suzie climbed back into her clothes and walked into town.

"Looking for nothing, miss?" said Sam.
Suzie kept walking. Something had caught
her eye. A familiar antiques shop.

"Oh, goody!" she said, looking around the room.
"What's for sale?"
"Uh, everything," said Otis.
Suzie pulled out her checkbook. "I'll take it."

It was almost five o'clock when the last things were carted away. Otis's shop was empty again. He was just about to close up when another customer walked in.

"Fantastic! What a super-duper shop you've got here!"
It was Tubby Portobello, the richest man in town.
"What's for sale?"

Otis checked the clock.
"Sorry, we're closed!"